Tommy Gallagher's Crusade

Books by James T. Farrell

A WORLD I NEVER MADE

NO STAR IS LOST

STUDS LONIGAN
A Trilogy, comprising
YOUNG LONIGAN · THE YOUNG MANHOOD OF
STUDS LONIGAN · JUDGMENT DAY

GAS-HOUSE McGINTY

CALICO SHOES

GUILLOTINE PARTY

CAN ALL THIS GRANDEUR PERISH?

A NOTE ON LITERARY CRITICISM

THE SHORT STORIES OF JAMES T. FARRELL

Tommy Gallagher's

Crusade BY JAMES T. FARRELL

———————————————————

THE VANGUARD PRESS · NEW YORK

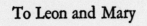
To Leon and Mary

The dog-star razes! nay, 'tis past a doubt,
All Bedlam, or Parnassus, is let out:
Fire in each eye, and papers in each hand,
They rave, recite, and madden round the land.

ALEXANDER POPE
Epistle to Dr. Arbuthnot

Tommy Gallagher's Crusade

1

"READ *Christian Justice!* Father Moylan's *Christian Justice,* ten cents a copy! See page three of this issue and learn what Father Moylan says of the Red menace. Get your *Christian Justice,* ten cents a copy!"

Tommy Gallagher stood on the curb in front of his parish church in Brooklyn, selling his magazines as the last Sunday mass let out. Tommy was a lad of twenty-five, husky, broad-shouldered, with a large round face with sensuous lips and dark brows which contributed to the ferocity of his expression when he frowned. The parishioners poured out of the church. Small knots of people gathered on the sidewalk to talk for a moment or two, while many others moved away.

Young fellows whom Tommy knew, some of them grammar school classmates of his, grinned at him. Now and then older people nodded, parishioners he had known for many years, friends of his mother and father. Most of the people were not interested in his magazine and passed him by. Several men faced him with unmistakable hostility but said nothing. A man of middle age in shabby clothes came up to him and bought a copy. The man said that Father Moylan was the real one for the common fellow. Tommy said sure he was. The man said that he had been out of work for two years, had been on relief, W.P.A., had looked for odd jobs, and he was fed up and felt that the only one who had spoken out for the poor devils like himself was Father Moylan. Tommy agreed. The man folded his copy of *Christian Justice* under his arm and walked on, a seedy, broken-looking figure.

"Read Father Moylan's *Christian Justice!* Ten cents a copy! Read *Christian Justice* and kick the Reds out of America!"

The crowd was almost gone now. Tommy stood there, hoping to make a last sale. He held up a copy of the magazine. It was printed in bold type, looked something like a newspaper, had large headlines and a picture on the front page. But he guessed that he'd have to call it quits. Jimmy Powers, a thin, over-dressed lad of Tommy's age, came over to him, smiling as he approached.

"What the hell, Tommy, when did you become a Red?" Jimmy asked.

"What's that?" Tommy retorted, taken by surprise.

"Ain't you a Red, selling magazines on the street?"

"Father Moylan's magazine! Read it and see what the Reds and the eagle-beaks are doin'," Tommy replied, holding up a copy.

"Oh! I thought it was only Reds and newsboys who sold magazines and papers on the streets."

"Here, Jimmy, buy one, it's only a dime."

"What'll I do with it?" Jimmy asked.

"Read it!"

"Sounds too much like work."

"Jimmy, it'll open your eyes. Come on, buy one,"

Tommy said, trying to thrust a copy into Jimmy's hand.

"Hell, Gallagher, *The Brooklyn Eagle* gives me enough readin' matter."

They were alone now in front of the church. Jimmy lit a cigarette. He offered Tommy one and held up a lighted match while Tommy lit his.

"Jimmy, you're a Christian and an American, ain't you?" Tommy asked.

"I guess so. And I'm a Dodger fan, too."

"Well, you ought to buy this magazine."

"Workin', Tommy?"

"I'm sellin'. Sellin' this," Tommy answered, and again he held up a copy.

"Hell, that ain't work," Jimmy said.

"I ain't ashamed of selling *Christian Justice*. You don't understand, Jimmy. Let me explain it to you."

"Explain what?"

"Oh, about Father Moylan and what he's doin'."

"I got to trot along. I got to get out to Ebbets Field early today if I want a seat. They're gonna pitch Van Lingle Mungo and I want to see the big boy come back. Tell me another time. Good luck, and hope you make a few pennies with your work there," Jimmy said, and he walked off.

Tommy looked after him, dour. He guessed he never liked that guy. He stuck his hands in his pockets and fingered his change. He'd only sold ten copies this morning. Hadn't made much dough. Well, he had about five bucks of his own. Maybe he'd have better luck next week. Carrying his bundle of magazines, he started toward home.

2

THE Gallagher family sat down to their Sunday dinner. The father was a lean man in his fifties with graying hair; for years he had worked for the telephone company as a repairman. A mild-mannered and genial man, he had never manifested much interest in politics. He had always voted the Democratic ticket and let it go at that. Mrs. Gallagher was a plump woman with lovely black hair that was beginning to streak with white. The oldest boy, Joe, was tall and lean like his father. He had a pretty good job working in the pay roll department of the telephone company. Bill was twenty-one, heavier and more burly than Tommy, with a jolly face and light hair. He was a clerk in an office in Manhattan and earned thirty dollars a week. All during the depression, Bill, Joe, and the father had been fortunate in retaining their jobs, and the family was comfortably enough situated to satisfy their normal wants.

The father and Joe had been talking about the telephone company and the dinner was progressing when Mrs. Gallagher suddenly looked at Tommy and said:

"I saw Mrs. Malone at early mass today. She was nice as pie, and told me that her son had a good job, and then she says she sees you in front of church every Sunday selling newspapers."

"He works for kikes. Catch me workin' for one of them eagle-beaks," Tommy blurted out.

"Why don't you say catch you working, and stop there?" Bill said, looking across the table at Tommy.

"Say, you punk, when you was still in school I had a job," Tommy countered.

"And you sure overworked yourself getting out of jobs and losing 'em ever since."

"Why don't you cut it out?" Mr. Gallagher asked.

"It seems to me that you ought to show a little

consideration for the rest of us. You ought to be able to get something better to do with that outfit you run around with besides selling newspapers," Joe said.

"I don't sell newspapers. I sell a magazine and I do it because it's my duty," Tommy answered.

Bill burst into hearty laughter.

"You talking about duty. You're gettin' so funny they ought to put you on the radio," Bill said.

Tommy glared at Bill. There was a dense expression on his face. He was trying to think of a quick comeback.

"That's what you say," Tommy finally said.

"Tommy, I don't know what's happening to you. You're gettin' touchy and always go around with a chip on your shoulder," Mr. Gallagher observed.

"I got my eyes opened," Tommy answered.

"And I'm gettin' mine open, too. Here Joe and I are saving our dough to get married, and he won't even look for a job," Bill said.

"How you gonna get a job when the Jewrocracy runs the country? Maybe if I had a name like Rosenstein, I'd have a good job."

20

"Well, why don't you change your name to Rosenstein then and get a job?"

No one spoke for a few moments, and they went on eating. Tommy was smouldering. He hadn't been able to think up anything to say to Bill's last crack.

"Tommy, the last time I went to a Holy Name Communion breakfast, I was talking to a young priest, Father Smith. He's a damned bright priest and well educated. I asked him about Father Moylan, and he said he couldn't go along with Father Moylan on this Jewish business, and it was going to give the Church a bad name. A priest shouldn't be mixing in politics like he does. If he does, what are the fellows on the other side of the fence gonna think?" Mr. Gallagher said.

"You don't understand," Tommy answered.

"Well, I'm tryin' to find out. Now, I used to think Father Moylan was all right, but when he turned against Roosevelt in the last election, that wasn't right. President Roosevelt is doin' the best he can, and if we pull along with him, he's goin' to get us out of all this mess."

21

"Rosenfeld," Tommy sneered.

"What's that?" Joe asked.

"I told you, Rosenfeld. And Mrs. Rosenfeld is a Red."

"Why, Mrs. Roosevelt is a lovely woman. I read her column every day in the newspaper, and it's wonderful," Mrs. Gallagher said.

"Tommy, that's no way to talk about the President of the United States and his wife," Mr. Gallagher reproached him.

"Hitler kicks the Jews out, and we make them governors of our states and let 'em walk all over us," Tommy said.

"Joe, what do you think he'll do when he takes over Roosevelt's job?" Bill asked sarcastically, nodding his head toward Tommy.

"Listen, you, I'm fed up with your insults!"

"Well, what you gonna do about it?" Bill asked, looking straight at Tommy.

"No fighting! Not in this family. This is a home not a street corner," the father interposed.

22

"That'll be news to him. He doesn't act like it was," Bill said.

"I told you, you punk!"

Bill jumped to his feet in anger and challenged:

"Try tellin' me with something besides that tongue of yours!"

Joe and the father were on their feet. Joe grabbed Bill and told him not to be doing anything rash. The father gazed from one to the other, disturbed.

Mrs. Gallagher banged on the table. They sat down and were quiet. Tommy ate hastily now. He pouted.

"There's going to be no more fighting at this table. Not while I'm alive," Mrs. Gallagher declared with determination.

"I didn't start it. Don't look at me," Tommy said.

Bill looked enigmatically at Tommy, smiled sardonically, said nothing.

"I don't know, but it seems to me we all ought to live and let live. That's my philosophy, and it's always been that. It's the same for the Jews as for everybody else. There's good and bad in all kinds.

23

We have too much fighting and hating in the world as it is, and the world is never going to get any better until it stops all this hating and fighting. We all got to make up our minds that we're gonna live and let live," Mr. Gallagher said.

Tommy looked arrogantly at his father. He was silent.

3

TOMMY GALLAGHER marched in the picket line carrying a sign which read:

FREE CHRISTIAN AMERICA FROM JEWRY

The line was moving back and forth in front of the entrance to a large building in the Fifties in which were located the offices of a radio station that had refused to sell Father Moylan time because of the priest's provocative addresses and because he had been widely charged with having made false statements.

There were about three hundred people in the picket line. It had been organized by the Association for Christian Freedom to which Tommy belonged.

He and many others in the line wore buttons on their coat lapels testifying to their membership in this organization. The main body of the demonstration consisted of young men, many of them unemployed. A number of them were dressed poorly; frayed collars and cuffs and an occasional shiny seat to a pair of trousers could be noticed in the moving line. The remainder of the crowd was mixed, including older men, girls, and corpulent women. Back and forth the line moved, going on the outside of the sidewalk by the curb, turning some distance down from the entrance to come back on the inside. In the crowd one could see fanatical faces, harried expressions, surly and sneering stares, sudden smiles. But the dominant mood of the demonstration was one of pugnacity. The crowd was spoiling for a fight. Policemen were lining the curb and were grouped at either end of the sidewalk area which the pickets covered. Passers-by and bystanders were hurried along, crowds and groups were not allowed to congregate. No magazine venders were permitted except those selling magazines to which the demonstrators were not hostile. Every now

and then a few persons would join the demonstration and a loud cheer of approval would sweep down
the marching line. In single file, they paraded back
and forth in front of the building entrance.

Tommy was thrilling with pride as he marched. In
front of him there was a little fellow with one elbow
almost out of his coat. He carried a sign which read:

FOR A CHRISTIAN AMERICA

What this little fellow lacked in size he made up
in voice, and at times even drowned out Tommy's
yells. The lad behind him was shorter than Tommy.
He was snappily dressed in a stylish suit with pleated
trousers. He had a pin-point mustache, and as he
marched, he constantly fingered it and smoothed
down his greasy black hair. He wore a button, and
carried a sign bearing the slogan:

BREAK THE RULE OF THE ATHEISTIC JEWS

Tommy kept looking at those passing in line on
the opposite side of the sidewalk. He nodded fre-
quently as he recognized faces of people he had met

27

at meetings of the Association. Spotting Al O'Reilley, he smiled and read the sign Al was carrying.

SMASH COMMUNISM

He walked in line, feeling a sense of unity with all these people. He felt that he was one with them, and that they were one with him, all ready to fight together. He thought what a fine sight it was to see this picket line of Christian Americans who had all come out like this in defense of Father Moylan.

A trim little girl of about eighteen, with blonde hair, passed on the opposite side and let out a screeching yell.

Twenty million Christians murdered in Russia!

Exercising all of his strong lung power, Tommy repeated her shout and was pleased when he got a smile from her. The yell spread up and down the line of marchers and it reverberated with increasing volume and swelling hatred. Again and again it was taken up and shrieked out.

Twenty million Christians murdered in Russia!

The slogan was dropped as suddenly as it had been

28

picked up. A sudden roar demanding free speech for
Father Moylan arose and died down. Tommy saw a
man with a red nose and gray hair swagger by,
carrying a picket sign which demanded:

KEEP AMERICA OUT OF WAR

He started thinking that if there were any attempt
to break this line, he would haul off and go swinging
into the center of the melee and more than one
dirty Red disrupter and hook-nose would know he'd
been hit.

The marchers began singsonging another slogan:
Free speech for Father Moylan!

Tommy reiterated the slogan without thinking of
what he was saying. Flashes of himself in the role
of a heroic street warrior, slugging the Reds and
Jews, kept coming and going in his mind. His arms
tired because of the sign he carried and he wished
that he were not lugging it in the demonstration.
Al O'Reilley went by again, and he noticed that Al
had gotten rid of his sign.

Tommy trudged along, and he thought how this

29

demonstration was bringing people together. This sense of unity thrilled him. And at the same time he wanted to stand out from these people and be noticed. He joined in a new cry, seeking to send his voice soaring above all the others.

Defend Catholic Mexico!

He walked self-consciously erect and flung back his head as he again exploded the new slogan. He ought to stand out from the shrimps ahead of and behind him. He threw back his shoulders and put on his fiercest frown. He walked now with his shoulders held back so tensely that the muscles of his back hurt, and his arm was tired from the weight of the sign. He watched out of the corner of his eye to see whether or not those passing him would look. He read a sign carried by a red-haired woman:

NO MORE CHRISTIAN MARTYRS TO RED ATHEISM

He frowned, grimaced, made faces. He had to relax his posture a little because he was fagging himself out by holding himself too firmly. No use wearing himself out this way because he'd need what it took if there was a fight. He marched on.

A swarthy girl in summery clothes that brought out her figure passed, and her sign read:

FREE SPEECH FOR FATHER MOYLAN AND
ALL CHRISTIAN AMERICANS

He'd like to know her.

Suddenly he noticed that there were newspaper photographers around taking pictures. Nearing two photographers, he contorted his features and let out a roaring demand for free speech for Father Moylan. He had hoped that they would snap him in action, and that then his picture would be in the newspapers tomorrow. But no pictures were taken when he passed the cameramen. He shuffled along, scraping his feet on the sidewalk. He looked at those opposite him, dragging along as if they were starting to get pooped out. It seemed as if many were now becoming weary of shouting. They walked more slowly, they yelled more sporadically, and they just drooped on. He hoped that the photographers would not go away before he passed them again.

"Snap it up. This ain't no way to walk," he said to the fellow in front of him.

"You tell 'em that. I can't go any faster than the one ahead of me."

He tramped along. A yell arose and spread up and down the line.

We demand free speech for Father Moylan!

But it soon faded out. The demonstration was losing its unity and its energy now. The slogans were being shouted out with only a momentary display of spirit.

Tommy again walked toward the photographers. He threw his shoulders back and held himself erect. But suppose that he were snapped and his picture did appear in the papers tomorrow morning, and the Reds saw it and recognized him, and then one day, he might be alone some place, walking along, minding his business, and they would remember him from the picture and pile on him? But no, that wasn't likely to happen. And he could take care of himself.

32

He could handle plenty of 'em. Everybody knew they were worms.

We demand free speech for Father Moylan!

The cry died out spiritlessly.

Like a speaker had said at one of the Association meetings, the Reds were all yellow. And yet it made him kind of afraid. Suppose five or ten of them jumped him? Just as he was thinking of this, he came in camera range, and the photographers were taking pictures. He averted his gaze without even exercising any volition; it was like a reflex action. He walked on, dragging his feet, and he began thinking how he hated the Jews and the Communists.

Buy Christian!

It was a girl who started this cry, and they took it up like a college crowd shouting a cheer.

Buy Christian! Buy Christian! Buy Christian!

The spirit of the marchers suddenly lifted as they chanted the slogan. They marched now, and many tried to keep step. And they kept up their chant.

Buy Christian! Buy Christian! Buy Christian!

But again they dropped their cry and straggled.

33

Tommy was now passing the cameras. He conquered his inclination to look away and looked bravely into the lenses, clenching his lips and holding the muscles of his face taut to seem tough. He walked on.

We demand free speech for Father Moylan!

The demonstration began to break up. Many were leaving it. There were gaps in the lines. Tommy remained in line until the crowd dispersed.

4

AFTER the demonstration had broken up, Al O'Reilley asked Tommy to come along with a couple of the fellows and have a drink. Tommy was introduced to them. Pete Sullivan was a burly young man wearing a shiny blue suit. Then he met Eddie Slavin, a skinny lad of about twenty-one with a pimply face, small and suspicious black eyes, and buck teeth. Tommy noticed that he had on a neat suit. He was glad that his own gray suit was still in good condition.

A fellow belonging to the Association was going to a parish house where they often met, and took the signs in his automobile, and that relieved them. They went over to a bar on Ninth Avenue, and sat together at a table having beer and sandwiches while a radio was blaring swing music, and several fellows lined up at the bar were talking knowingly about prize fighters. They were enthusiastic and excited because of the demonstration and talked about it for a while, and then they got to talking about jobs.

"I'm in slavery," Eddie Slavin exclaimed.

"You're lucky," Pete Sullivan said.

"You wouldn't think so if you had my job. I'm a doorman in an apartment hotel down near Washington Square. The bastards make me work ten hours a day, and with the little dough I get, one of the guys there is trying to steam me up to join a goddamn union and pay 'em dues," Eddie said.

"Is the guy a Red?"

"I guess so. I see him comin' to work and goin' home with books under his arm, and he acts like a screwball," Eddie said.

"If you need any help, just say the word, boy," Al remarked.

"Boy, am I fed up! Some of the people livin' in the place are fine people, but then, others aren't. Christ, there's one damned bitch who's always belly-

36

aching about me. And most of the people who come
to see her got noses that make me suspicious. And
goddamn it, I don't see why I, a freeborn white
American, have to be a flunky for Jews, open doors
and elevators for 'em, say yes sir and yes ma'm to
'em, run their goddamn errands, take crap from
sheenies. I tell you, I'm fed up," Eddie Slavin went
on. With a resolute gesture he lifted his glass of
beer and took a drink.

"You're a lucky bastard, Al, with your old man
doing good," Pete said.

"Me and Father Moylan are O.K. with my old
man. He likes what I do and says it's for the good
of the country," Al explained.

"You know, my old man just can't get anything
into his head. He thinks I'm a screwball," Tommy
complained.

"Well, I'm fed up, boys, and so is the old man.
He had a hat store out in Flushing and he was doin'
good, and then with bad times it went kerflooie, and
he's on his ear now. He works for the W.P.A. and
he's always down in the mouth," Pete said.

"You want to explain to him what's wrong, tell him it's the Jews," Al told Pete.

"I got it figured out that if there weren't so many dames working, why, guys like us would be better off," Eddie Slavin said.

"That's why Hitler told the dames to stay home where they belong and have babies, and let the men work," Al declared.

"Say, Slavin, any chance of my gettin' a job where you are?" Pete asked.

"Gee, I don't know. They're full up, but guys are always comin' and goin'. If there's any chance, I'll tip you off."

"Do, will yuh," Pete urged.

"Sure I will. Only it's one goddamn lousy job, if you want to know."

"I don't care. I'm fed up," Pete said.

Tommy thought to himself that they could just catch him being a doorman and wearing a flunky's uniform. Catch him!

They had another round of beers.

Pete told a story he'd heard about the Reds and

38

their girl friends, and they discussed girls. When they finished their beer, they paid their checks. Pete Sullivan said he was lucky he could pay his share. He'd had a pretty good week selling *Christian Justice*. They left and walked four abreast over to Eighth Avenue.

Tommy wanted something exciting to happen. He felt a kind of letdown after the afternoon's activity. He wanted girls, drinking, fun, action. He remembered how often he had felt just like this, having nothing to do, and wanting a little fun and excitement, and how he'd cruised around with guys he knew, looking for something to happen, and nothing had, and he'd gone home feeling that another night had gone down the sewer. He was kind of afraid that tonight might be the same. All his life, he'd had a feeling that something big was going to happen to him, and it never had. Since he'd gotten interested in Father Moylan and joined the Association for Christian Freedom, this feeling had gotten stronger in him. And damn it, life had gotten more exciting. He had things to do that gave him a feeling of his

39

own place in the world that he'd never had before. Yes, he had the feeling now more than ever that something big was going to come to him that he'd never had before and that he'd always wanted and waited for.

They turned onto Eighth Avenue and heard the rumbling of the subway underneath the sidewalk. A few feet ahead, Tommy saw a couple strolling toward him, and both were clearly Semitic. The fellow was smaller than Tommy, and the girl was good-looking and had a nice figure outlined by her dress.

"Close ranks, boys!" Tommy said quickly and under his breath.

They linked arms. The couple came face to face with them, surprised to find their path blocked by four sneering, tough-looking young men. The Jewish fellow was taken aback. The girl clung to his arm and her lips trembled.

"Lots of sidewalk out there," Tommy said curtly, pointing beyond the curb.

The fellow and girl tried to go around Tommy on the right, and a few pedestrians paused to watch what was happening. Tommy and his companions moved over.

"Get out on the street and make it fast!" Eddie Slavin yelled.

The Jewish lad blanched. He moved over to the curb, stepped off, walked with the girl on the street for a few feet, and then regained the sidewalk. The four boys laughed heartily, and spectators didn't know what was happening. The Jewish lad and his girl were lost in the crowd. Tommy and the boys walked on, laughing.

"Before we finish, boys, there won't be a Jew in New York," Tommy boasted.

They walked on. Pete Sullivan remarked that the two Hebes were lucky they didn't get worse. Tommy looked dour. He wanted excitement. Maybe a fight! With the others along, it wouldn't be too dangerous. No, he wanted it to be dangerous. And he knew himself that he didn't want this. And knowing it himself, it filled him with hate and envy.

"How about another beer, boys?" Al suggested.

41

5

FEELING low, Tommy woke up and saw that it was already eleven o'clock. He got out of bed but felt dizzy. He went back to bed and turned his eyes away from the light. Lying down, he felt all right. He tried to remember last night. They'd gone to several bars, and he recalled how he'd almost gotten into a fight in one of them. But he couldn't remember clearly just what had happened.

He was going over to New York to sell the magazine on the street, but he could stay in bed a little while longer and go down in the afternoon. He had to sell, too, because he was broke. He'd spent all his dough last night. He dozed off to sleep and awakened a half hour later. He lay in bed, attracted by his own imaginings of his fighting ability, and he began knocking Jews and Reds all over in his mind. He dozed off to sleep in the midst of his fantasy and got up at twelve-thirty, feeling a little better for the extra sleep.

He got dressed and went out into the kitchen for breakfast. His mother didn't say a word to him. He was hoping she wouldn't be sore because he didn't want to be quarreling with her.

"Hello, Mom," he said with forced cordiality.

"Up late, Tommy," she answered.

"I know, Mom. I didn't get in early last night."

"Neither did your brother Bill, but he was up bright and early this morning and over to work at his office."

"He's lucky. He's got a decent job."

"You'll never find a decent job if you go out looking for it at this time of day."

"I've been looking for jobs so long, I'm fed up."

"Whenever you had jobs, you lost them."

"It wasn't my fault. I ain't responsible for conditions. And then, at most of my jobs they never liked

43

me. The last place, the boss was against me. How can you have a job when the boss is against you for no good reason?"

"Sit down and have your breakfast," she said.

He dropped into a chair at the kitchen table. He remembered that he didn't have a red cent. He'd have to ask her for money again. He'd been a damned fool for not getting up early, because then it'd have been easier to get something off her. But he couldn't have done it, feeling like he did. He was still low and nervous and breaking out with sudden fits of sweating. But he'd get over it. A bigger problem was how he was going to ask her for money.

"Gee, Mom, you don't have to act so sore at me," he complained in a whining, injured voice when his mother set coffee and toast before him.

"I'm not angry with you," she replied curtly.

"Well, gee, what's the matter then?"

"Eat your breakfast. I've got lots to do. We can't afford servants in this house," she said, leaving the kitchen.

He sat munching toast and drinking coffee. He lit

44

a cigarette. He only had a few left, and didn't even have the price of another pack. He felt sorry for himself. He was getting a raw deal. He had never had a decent job in his life. Most of the jobs he'd had were lousy and he'd had to go to work and ride in the subways in dirty old work clothes while others went to work and came home dressed up. They were all against him. Mom was treating him like a stepson. They were all against him, and they didn't understand.

Sulking, he finished his cup of coffee, went to the stove and poured another, and came back to the table and sat down with it. He still sulked.

He broke out in another sweat. He felt weak. Gee, how was he going to get through the day? And how was he going to get any money from Mom when she seemed so sore at him?

His coffee was lukewarm. He dumped the cup in the sink.

6

IT WAS a sunny afternoon in the middle of the week. Tommy stood on the corner opposite the New York Public Library at Forty-second Street and Fifth Avenue selling *Christian Justice*. He had a good position, but near-by were three girls selling a magazine hostile to Father Moylan. Four cops stood around to prevent trouble. There had been a small riot on the same corner only two days before, but Tommy hadn't been there that day. Today it was quiet. The presence of the cops made Tommy feel more at ease. Several of the boys were supposed to have come around to protect him in case there was any trouble. But they hadn't shown up, and he'd given up hope now that they would come. But any-

46

way, they wouldn't be needed when there were only girls around selling that magazine.

"Anti-Semitism is un-American!" the girl selling the magazine cried to the passers-by, while her two companions stood at her side.

Tommy called out his magazine, holding up a copy. He tried to watch the girls out of the corner of his eye, but people kept getting in his way. He wanted to see if they were selling more than he was. The girls didn't look Jewish, and the one with the magazines in her hand was pretty, with dark hair, a slim figure, and nice legs. She looked as if she might even be Irish. He couldn't seem to keep his eyes off her. She was more than good-looking enough to date up.

"Read Father Moylan's *Christian Justice!* Read it and see who are un-American and un-Christian! Read *Christian Justice!* Father Moylan's *Christian Justice,* ten cents a copy. Get *Christian Justice* and kick the Reds out of America!" he cried out.

"Yes, and kick Father Moylan out with them," a

middle-aged woman screamed at him as she walked by. A cop frowned but said nothing.

Tommy scowled after the woman.

There was a steady flow of people along the sidewalk. A number hastened or drifted by without paying attention to any of the venders. Others strolling along paused to look at the girls and at Tommy, stood gaping for a few moments, and then passed on. Whenever too many people collected and remained too long to watch, the cops told them curtly to break it up and move on. Now and then pedestrians stopped to talk to the cops, to ask questions, and to protest about one or another of the magazine sellers.

"Go on back to Russia," a well-dressed man with a sleek shiny face said to Tommy.

"Read Father Moylan and toss the Reds out of America," Tommy yelled quickly.

A man halted and stood gazing at Tommy. He was powerfully built and looked as if he were a Swede. He said nothing. He placed his hands on his

48

hips and stared. Tommy was so disconcerted that he could not meet this stranger's cold blue eyes.

"*Christian Justice,* ten cents a copy," Tommy cried out rather weakly, so disturbed by the man that he toned down his sales cry.

Tommy tried to appear busy and unaware of him. Suddenly he was drawn to look directly at him. The man sneered. He spat on the sidewalk. He walked on. Tommy looked after him.

"Another Red sonofabitch!" he muttered to himself. He scowled ferociously.

"Hitler kicks 'em out. Read what we do for 'em in *Christian Justice!*" he bawled out, holding a copy aloft.

A passing girl gave him a smile. He smiled after her and wished she'd said something, or he'd had something on the tip of his tongue to say to attract her. Maybe standing here, a swell-looking girl would pick him up. He wandered off in his thoughts and forgot to call out his magazine. Suddenly he looked down and saw the black-haired girl selling a copy.

"Twenty million Christians murdered in Spain,

49

Russia, and Mexico. Read *Christian Justice!*" he barked.

A little fellow came up to him.

"Why do you do this?" the little fellow asked in a sad voice.

"Huh?"

"Why do you spread the fires of race hatred like this, young fellow?" the man asked.

"Scram!" Tommy said.

The man walked off, shaking his head. Tommy stood there, scowling, grimacing, barking out his cries, feeling to himself that if he looked tough as hell, it would make them afraid, and that was half the battle won. But he wasn't making many sales. He'd only sold about nine copies. He glanced down at the girls. They seemed to be selling some, but he didn't know how many.

And the endless crowd filed past Forty-second Street and Fifth Avenue, and the steady stream of traffic poured by. He was getting fed up. His arm was beginning to tire from holding up the maga- zine. He shifted his bundle to his right arm and held a copy before his chest with his left hand. It seemed as if at least a half hour went by without a sale. One person after another passed, either not seeing him or else looking at him with a hasty, apathetic glance. Out of the corner of his eye he saw the girl sell another copy. He clenched his teeth. Someone ought to tear the damned rag out of her hand and slap her face.

"Why don't you get a job, you bum?" a passing woman yelled at him.

"I will when you Jews are thrown out of America," he yelled after her.

"I'm a better American than you are," she retorted.

"Read *Christian Justice* and save America," he barked.

"Bum!" the woman said before passing on.

A well-dressed man gave Tommy a dime. Tommy handed him the magazine and said thanks. The man casually moved off, tearing the magazine up and tossing the scraps in a large wire basket used as a public trash receptacle. Tommy cursed and grimaced.

And the crowd flowed by. No more sales.

"Here you are, Father Moylan's *Christian Justice,*
only magazine in America telling the truth about
international bankers. Read *Christian Justice* and
smash the Reds! Ten cents a copy!"

And suddenly he was finding out that he could
not check himself from looking down at the black-
haired girl.

"Read it! Read it! Here you are, read it, a defense
of American morality, *Christian Justice!*"

She was taking all his business away, and for what?
To sell a filthy Communist rag!

The crowd passed on. Few people now showed
any interest in either magazine vender. Neither
Tommy nor the girl was making many sales. And
the crowd passed them in an endless stream.

"Read *Christian Justice!*"

"Anti-Semitism is un-American!"

7

"JOE, here's the newsboy," Bill remarked when Tommy got home.

Tommy didn't answer. He went to his room and left his magazines in the closet, and then came to the living room.

"Extry paper! Read it and save the world! Read it and weep!"

"Sell any papers today, Tom?" Bill asked.

"What's it to you?"

"From newsboy to dictator," Joe said.

"You guys mind your own business," Tommy said curtly. He walked across the room and stood looking out of the window, his eyes fastened vacantly on the red brick two-story building across the street. Once a sweet girl named Mary Cecilia Connor had lived there, and he had used to sit here and watch for her to come out and had thought of her a lot and of how he would like to take her out and be in love with her, and he had never gotten beyond a nodding acquaintance with her. Her family had moved out to Jackson Heights, and he'd never heard anything about her again. She had been a nice girl, and he was suddenly nostalgic, nostalgic for the days when he would sometimes see her come out of that building, and sometimes pass her on the street and say hello. He finally turned from the window and glared at his brothers.

"Aw, let him alone," Bill said, winking at Joe.

"You guys mind your own goddamn business," Tommy snapped.

"Didn't I tell you to let him alone?" Bill said.

"And you too, shut your mouth!"

Scowling, he stamped out of the room. Both brothers laughed.

8

"THEY didn't build America! The Christian built America!" the lean baldish speaker said in his deep bass voice, drawing a roar of applause from the one hundred and fifty odd persons attending the meeting in the little hall on Third Avenue in the Sixties.

He paused and looked dramatically at his audience, which consisted mainly of young fellows like Tommy and middle-aged women. Just as the shouts died down, an elevated train rumbled by outside, drowning out the voices within. Behind the speaker there was a banner of the Christian American Party, a small political organization under whose auspices the meeting was being held. It was part of the Association

55

for Christian Freedom. Around the hall there were signs and banners calling for the destruction of the Red Menace and for the freedom and prosperity of Christian America. The speaker was the last one on the evening's program, a man from out of town. The previous speakers had worked up the audience for him, so that when he had begun, he had them in a frenzied mood, ready to yell and applaud almost his every sentence. And he had played upon them and was now going along full steam, with the audience having become almost a unit in its cheering, roaring, hissing, catcalling, and yelling as the appropriate stimuli were issued.

Tommy sat near the exit in a row of camp chairs, and beside him were young men, all wearing the Association button. Tommy was slouched a bit in his chair, and there was a faraway look on his face.

"*They* didn't do the pick and shovel work to make America what it is today. Oh, no, not *they!*" the speaker said, emphasizing his words with a heavy and obviously sarcastic tone of voice.

Again he paused while he heard sarcastic laughter.

Tommy's face seemed to light up with sudden interest, and he sat erect and attentive.

"It was the Christian who did the pick and shovel work to build America!" the speaker yelled, accompanying his words with flourishing gestures.

The audience roared agreement. Tommy thought that this was true, and told himself that since it was, why should Christians, Christians like himself, have to do the pick and shovel work today? Why should he have to take a laborer's job and ride in the subway in dirty clothes and let everybody see he couldn't be any better than a common workman? Let *them* do that!

As the applause died down, a stout woman with a pudgy face yelled in a loud voice:

"Name them!"

"My fellow Christians, I don't have to name *them*," the speaker replied, smiling unctuously.

A lean woman, whose face was beginning to crack with wrinkles, jumped to her feet.

"I'll name them!" she cried in a shrill, high-pitched voice. "I'll name them! The dirty *Jews!*"

57

"Hear! Hear!" a red-faced little Irishman shouted.

There were many boos and catcalls.

"Down with the Jews!" Tommy boomed.

"Up the Gentile!" the red-faced little Irishman shouted.

"Down with the kikes!" Tommy boomed, but an elevated train drowned out his cry.

The speaker stood poised, and when he could proceed he smiled knowingly.

"Far be it from me, my fellow Christians, to be an anti-Semite," he said suavely, and many of the audience laughed good-naturedly. He continued. "Anti-Semite is now the gutter phrase which the Reds use to cast scorn on those who would do their Christian and patriotic duty."

More boos and catcalls.

"I am not afraid of the word when aliens, Reds, hook-nosed parasites hurl it at me," he cried out in a rising voice. "No, when I am called that by such ilk, it is a badge of honor. When they call me that, they prove that I am not veering from the right course."

58

He paused to receive an outburst of cheers.

"Down with the Reds!" Tommy shouted with all his lung power, and his cry was taken up.

"I am not here to talk against this race or that," the speaker continued. "I am here to talk about American conditions, about the problems which are facing Christian America in its gravest and darkest hour of peril."

More cheers.

"My fellow Christians, what has America come to when a man of God, a clergyman, a great American, a great Christian, a champion of the common people, is barred from speaking over the radio in the name of justice because he tells the truth?" He waited for the catcalls, hisses, and boos. "Why is he barred from the radio?"

"Ask the Jews!" a woman screamed.

"Why is he barred? Because he tells the truth."

The audience cheered hysterically, rising to its feet, climbing on the chairs, drowning out the rumble of another passing elevated train. Tommy was on his chair, yelling until he was hoarse and out of breath.

"He tells the truth, and certain gentlemen, so-called, do not like to hear the truth. And, my Christian friends, I might add that these gentlemen are not named Murphy, or Gallagher, or O'Reilley. No, they aren't named Smith or Jones, either."

He paused for another reverberating catcall.

"But what of it? Do these gentlemen, so-called, care for the truth? Ask me another. Do the rulers of Red Russia care for the truth?"

"Save America from the Jews!" a red-haired woman screamed, and many took up her cry, shouting it in unison.

"Save America! Yes, my Christian compatriots, save America! Save America from all the enemies within her gates!" he shouted with the practiced inflection of one who knew how to mold his audience. And then he waited for the proper response of assent. Another elevated train interfered with this assent, and then he was able to continue.

"But America will be saved!"

Roars.

"And America will be Christian!"

60

Hysterical roars.

"Last week," the speaker continued in a lower key, "I spoke in Philadelphia, and six hundred people joined our party, six hundred Christian Americans."

The audience once more was on its feet, exploding all its lung power in enthusiastic greeting of this announcement. Tommy, once more on his chair, was shouting and thinking of how things were moving, and he was thrilling with the sense of belonging to something that was growing in power and numbers.

"Two weeks ago, I spoke in Chicago. Two thousand joined us." The speaker produced another wave of cheers. "Two thousand Christian Americans who see eye to eye with us."

From without came the sirens of fire engines, and the hall seemed like a bedlam.

"Tremble, Judea!" a tall, emaciated woman cried, standing on a chair and waving bony arms.

She was cheered. The fire engine sirens were heard again. The tall woman was waving her arms and lost her balance, but as she fell from the chair,

61

two men caught her. Tommy and some of the other young men laughed.

"My friends, our movement is greater than the Crusades. It is the New Crusade."

More noise.

Poised and waiting, his face beaming with smiles, the speaker watched the audience seethe. He casually poured water from the pitcher on the table beside him, took up a glass, drank.

"And that reminds me," he went on, smiling disingenuously, his voice in a low key. "That reminds me." They knew something was coming, and waited. "Where did the Crusaders go in the Crusades of the Middle Ages?"

"Jewrusalem," a woman yelled, and many parroted her, and there was much laughter.

"And the new crusaders are coming to Jew York," the red-haired woman yelled.

"Down with the Jews of Jew York!" Tommy boomed.

"That reminds me of something funny that happened to me when I came to this town to make my

62

speech here. You know, when I came in, the custom inspector stopped me, and I had trouble smuggling in my Bible with the New Testament. And I had forgotten my passport. You know, coming here, I forgot that I was coming into a foreign country."

There was more laughter; then hisses, boos, and more catcalls.

He went on. Tommy felt that he wanted to be in with everybody here, to yell with them, boo with them, shout out cries which would make them laugh and yell, and make them turn and look at him, see that he'd made them laugh and yell, feel that they liked it and respected him and thought he was all right and regular. The speaker continued. Tommy suddenly wasn't listening. He remembered how when he'd been a kid in school, he would always find himself not able to listen to what was said, and sometimes now he found he still couldn't listen for a long time. He leaned forward in his chair and told himself that he would listen. He kept thinking and telling himself now what could his family say if they knew all this, heard and saw this here tonight, came

63

here? And how could the Reds answer this man? What would people say who insulted him, gave him dirty looks, made dirty cracks at him when he stood on the street selling the magazine? What would they say if they were here tonight?

"If *they* did not control the press, the radio, Hollywood, even some of the highest offices in the land, then, then the Christians of this country would know of the danger facing them. But *they* do control so much that they pull the wool over the eyes of the decent Christians of America. And it is the old, old story. *They* have climbed on the backs of others, and it is to *their* interest that the truth be strangled and treated with contempt, that the truth be denied to the Christians of this country."

Tommy was still leaning forward, attentive, straining and forcing himself to listen to every word. And he reminded himself that he would have to remember some of the things this man said and use them when he was out selling *Christian Justice.*

The speaker went on, describing plots and revolutionary schemes to drench America in blood and turn it into a Soviet state. These plots were being hatched in Mexico, and a Red Army was being organized to march into America and to turn it into another Spain, another Russia, another Mexico. He said that, in fact, these other countries had only provided the dress rehearsals for the terror now being planned for America.

"If *they* have *their* way, *they* will get more than Shylock's pound of flesh!" he shouted.

"Kill *them*. Kill the Jews! Kill the Reds!" a hysterical woman shouted, and her cry was taken up fanatically.

By the time the speaker had finished, there was a unified mood of hostility and fanaticism pervading those present. Tommy was stirred. He wanted to strike a blow immediately for the cause the speaker had glorified. He was afraid, too. At times during the evening he and many others had trembled when the speaker had described what the Reds would do if their revolution succeeded. He had even imagined himself being tortured, torn limb from limb by Reds.

He wanted to see them stopped before they got too powerful, and perhaps it was too late already.

With the meeting over, women were crowded around the speaker. A neat well-dressed man with a mustache was signing up seven recruits to the party, and literature was being sold at a table by the exit door. Tommy stood indecisive. He wanted to go up and tell the speaker he was with him, give him his name, bring himself to the attention of the speaker. Just as he started up, Al O'Reilley came up to him.

"Doin' anything, Gallagher?"

"Why?"

"Give him some of the stickers, Frank," Al said.

A dark-browed fellow handed Tommy stickers on which was printed the slogan BUY CHRISTIAN. Tommy took them.

"We're goin' out to paste these around," Al said.

"Can you wait a minute?" Tommy asked.

"Why? What for?"

"I wanted to go up and say a word to the speaker," Tommy answered.

66

"Come on, do it another time. We got to get busy. It's gettin' late," Al snapped at him.

Disappointed that he was missing the chance to make himself known to the speaker, Tommy left with Al and six others.

They went along Third Avenue, pasting their signs on darkened store windows and elevated posts. They bumped into a lone fellow with a large nose and Semitic features. Tommy and Al clouted him in the face, and the fellow was knocked groggy and unable to defend himself. They surrounded him, jeered him as a Jew, and punched him some more. Al laughed while Tommy pasted a sticker on his coat. Then Al gave him a kick and told him to beat it. The man staggered away. One of the fellows found an old tomato, and whizzed it after him, but missed. They hooted until the Jew was out of sight, and went on pasting up their stickers.

When they reached Fourteenth Street, they had used up all they had. They walked over to Union Square, making dirty cracks as they walked. At Union Square there was a small group on a street corner

discussing politics. The boys busted into the group
and began arguing. The group was dispersed by cops.
One of the fellows, with a Yiddish accent, demanded
that the cops arrest Tommy and his pals, and the cop
told him that he had better blow, and blow quickly.
The cop then told Tommy and the boys to watch
their step in this neighborhood with all the Reds
around. Al said that he knew of a school run by the
Socialist Party, more Reds, near by, that they ought
to do a job on. They made their way to an old loft
building on a dark street off Union Square.

9

TOMMY, Al O'Reilley, and a number of the boys had been going around, starting street fights with persons whose features were clearly Semitic, and breaking up street meetings. They had usually been successful in these tactics. They had had fun, and had escaped serious injuries. Al and Pete Sullivan had been arrested, and in court. The judge had warned them to stop and count fifty before they got into any more fights, and then let them go. This had made them heroes, and Tommy had envied them their honors. When they broke up street meetings, they used a regular technique. They would saunter up to a meeting in twos and threes and place themselves strategically in the crowd, with a number of them up in front to be in a good position to rush the speaker and beat him up. Before they would get down to the serious business of bruising and punching, they would first try to disrupt the meeting, frighten the speaker and listeners, and make their work easier by a preliminary process of demoralization. They would mill about, push and shove, step on toes, heckle, interrupt, and boo.

On a pleasant Saturday evening, a number of them took a subway up to the Bronx, planning to break up a street meeting. They had broken one up at the same corner two weeks previously, manhandling a number of the listeners and slugging the speaker. Tommy had carried off honors in this fray. He had moved about during the fracas doling out rabbit punches in the back of the neck that had had telling effects. They had learned that despite their work, meetings were still being held in the same place, and they decided to drive them off that corner for good.

It was a corner by a vacant lot in a workers' district, and there were small brick buildings along both sides of the street. The speaker stood on a stand from

which an American flag drooped. This evening the
speaker was a gray-haired man with a rich, full voice.
The crowd was larger than it had been on the night
the boys had broken up the meeting. A number of
the crowd appeared to be workingmen, but a still
larger proportion were youths, radical lads and girls,
many of whom were students. There was also a
good sprinkling of the inquisitive, those people who
look at building construction going on, watch fires,
listen to harangues from soap boxes just in order to
pass the time. Some of the youths looked pretty burly
and they were to be found in the crowd in groups,
one group of ten or twelve standing directly before
the speaker's stand. Only ten fellows had come along
to break up the meeting: Al O'Reilley, Tommy, Pete
Sullivan, Eddie Slavin, a little fellow named Johnny
Brown, and five bruisers whom Tommy didn't know.
Coming up on the subway, they had had a lot of fun
kidding with Pete and Al about counting fifty before
they hauled off on a Red or crashed their fists into
an eagle-beak. They sauntered up to the meeting in
the usual fashion, but since there were fewer of them

than they had expected and the crowd was a little large, they stuck close together on the right wing of the crowd. Before they had come, there had been some bitter heckling of the meeting, coming from a group of Communists. The speaker had countered the hecklers, and finally they had marched off in dudgeon after calling on all workers assembled to shun this Trotskyite meeting like a plague. After they left, the meeting proceeded in an orderly fashion. Gradually, people out strolling had stopped to listen. When Tommy arrived, he gazed about with an apprehensive look, because there was a bigger crowd than he had counted on. The first words that he heard were:

"When the Fascists rear their heads here, only the revolutionary working class can smash them and liberate all mankind from fascism and capitalism. Comrades, fellow workers, friends, this is the lesson of revolutionary defeats suffered in Europe, and this is the lesson we must learn in America before it is too late."

Tommy grinned. The usual boushwah of the Reds,

he reflected. He thought how he might be arrested, and get out scot free, and that would be something to raise his stock. He smiled to himself, wondering what the family would think if he got pinched.

"That is why we have issued calls for a Workers Defense Guard to be prepared to smash the Fascist gangs when they raise their heads in America as they have begun to do," the speaker went on.

Tommy frowned. What did this bastard mean? Well, in a couple of minutes he'd eat his words, and maybe he'd eat them along with a couple of his own teeth that would be knocked down his throat. He looked around. The crowd was growing, and some of those around liked what this Red louse was saying. He noticed, too, that a number of Jews were listening. And some of the Jews, he reflected, said that the Jews weren't Red. Well, they were. And still, there were some big guys around here. Well, maybe it was just as he heard speakers say at meetings, the Reds had no guts. And again he glanced around. Some of the guys here were pretty husky.

"Let's get going," Al whispered to Tommy.

73

"They ain't worth smacking down, these bums," Tommy said quietly to Al.

"What's the matter, gettin' yellow?" Al answered in a low voice, and all the while the speaker was continuing his harangue, launching into an attack on Father Moylan.

"Who's yellow?"

"Well, why did you make that crack?" Al said.

"They're punks," Tommy said.

"Punks or not, we're gonna get 'em! Now, let's start grinding the organ. Start yelling out at 'em," Al said.

Neither of them observed that they were being closely watched, and that a group of youths and men edged through the crowd and stood near them.

"Comrades, you know the Moylanites broke up our last meeting. Comrades . . ."

"Litvinov's name is Bronstein and Trotsky's is Finklestein," Tommy yelled.

He had blurted it out before he knew exactly what he was saying. He trembled now, and he was nervous. But this would show that he wasn't yellow.

74

"Get down off there, Finklestein!" a husky yelled.

"Quit hidin' behind the flag, Finklestein!" Al O'Reilley yelled.

There was movement in the crowd. Some started edging away. Others, mainly youths, began going over toward the hecklers.

"Do not let yourself be provoked, comrades! Defend yourselves and your meeting if attacked," the speaker yelled.

People around Al, Tommy and the others were telling them to shut up. Near Tommy, an argument about Americanism broke out. A tall Slav with a foreign accent told the Moylanite boys to shut up and leave the meeting.

"This is a free country, and we're Americans," Eddie Slavin replied to him.

There was a tension pervading the meeting now, but suddenly the audience was quiet, and the speaker was going on.

"Who is this sanctimonious hypocrite who bellows Fascism over the radio?" the speaker said, raising his voice.

"Don't say that again, you!" Tommy bellowed.

"Quit hidin' behind the flag!" Al yelled.

The tall Slav told them that they should shut up or leave the meeting. Arguments were breaking out in the crowd, and the speaker couldn't be heard.

"Quit hidin' behind the flag!" Al O'Reilley yelled again.

All his companions started shouting this cry in unison. Somebody was pushed. Someone had his toe stepped on. A girl yelled. There were scuffles. Pete Sullivan suddenly rushed a youth and they traded blows. Tommy saw Al O'Reilley slip on brass knuckles and cut the jaw of a fellow in a blue shirt. Tommy caught the fellow off balance and clipped him on the other jaw. The fellow's knees sagged. The fighting was general. The crowd opened up, and there was slugging on all sides, curses, screams, yells. Many who had stopped to listen hurried away, while others stepped aside and watched. The youths near the stand closed in on Tommy and his companions.

Tommy moved to polish off a little Jew in front of him. Just as he took a step forward with fists

cocked, he was smashed in the left eye. He seemed
to see streaks of irregular light. He felt a sharp pain
in his eye. He had a sick thudding headache. His
whole body seemed to grow weak and powerless. He
bent forward, holding his eye. He was pounded on
the face until he dropped. He moaned.

Everything now was like a nightmare to him.
Curses, cries, angry taunts, screams, groans, swinging
fists, clashing bodies were all about him. His head
cleared a little. He noticed there was blood on his
hands. He tried to rise and he was knocked down.
Groggy, he staggered off to one side.

Al O'Reilley was backing away with a welt on his
cheek. Pressing him was a broad-shouldered worker
whose face was streaming blood, but who came at
him pumping his hands like dynamos. Al swung out
but not so swiftly as his opponent, and the broad-
shouldered laborer sent him spinning backward.
Eddie Slavin, his shirt ripped half off, suddenly
bolted out of the crowd and ran lickety-split down
the street.

Women were screaming, and spectators were yelling for the police to come. People came running down the street from the near-by houses.

"Kill the Fascists!" many began to cry.

"Inhuman, barbarous," a man watching was saying.

"Is this democracy, heh?" a Jewish man with gray hair said on the sidelines.

All those who had come with Al and Tommy to disrupt the meeting were backing off. Tommy's head had cleared a little. He was like a sick animal. He could feel his eye swelling. He saw the brawling and slugging with his good eye. It looked bad for the boys. He slunk away from the fighting.

Al and the other boys continued to retreat, taking severe punishment. They were now outnumbered, and the defenders of the meeting fought with fury. A young Jewish boy yelled, "Down with Fascism," and rushed headlong at Pete Sullivan. Pete caught him coming in, square on the jaw with an uppercut. The boy half turned from the force of the blow, and his knees gave way. He dropped on the street, uncon-

78

scious. Pete was smashed in the nose. He turned and ran off. Police sirens were heard. Al and all the others beat it down the street, followed by taunts, angry cries, and a few flying bricks.

10

"BOY, your face looks like a slow-motion sunset," Bill said.

Tommy frowned. He looked grotesque. There was a yellowish, purplish-black spot around his left eye, covering the swollen lid and circling down under the eye. The eye was bloodshot and watered constantly so that while he ate, he had to keep dabbing at it with a handkerchief. He found also that he could not chew on the left side without his jaw hurting.

"Let him alone," Mr. Gallagher said.

"He's got it coming to him. He goes around telling us we don't understand, as if he knew something. He had it coming to him, the hoodlum," Joe spoke up.

"It wasn't a hoodlum fight," Tommy said.

Mr. Gallagher looked pained.

80

"All I want to say is I'm fed up with him. Why doesn't he get a job and not expect others to feed him?" Bill said.

"Tommy, I hope you learned your lesson. You might get killed going out this way," Mr. Gallagher added.

"I swear I don't know what the world's coming to, with this fighting. And when I saw him Sunday morning, I thought I was seeing a ghost," Mrs. Gallagher exclaimed.

"Or a cartoon for Ripley's," Bill said.

Tommy glared at Bill. His eye watered. He dabbed it with his handkerchief. He felt humiliated.

"Well, he wasn't only afraid to be the newsboy yesterday morning in front of church. He was afraid to go to mass for fear somebody would see that interior decorating on his face," Bill said.

"I can take it, don't worry about me. And let me tell you, the kikes will pay for this."

"Tommy, why don't you cut this stuff out and try and get a job? You know there's no good in all this fighting, no good is ever going to come of it. I don't

81

care what you say you're fighting for, it's no good. You got to learn to live and let live, and if you do, the other fellow'd be the same to you," Mr. Gallagher said.

"Maybe you want to have 'em walk all over you. Well, I don't," Tommy answered.

Joe and Bill burst into laughter.

"You sure look like you got stepped on and tramped over," Bill said.

Tommy jumped from his chair and stalked out of the room. His mother followed him, while Joe and Bill told each other that nobody should give him sympathy now, because he'd gotten what was coming to him. Mrs. Gallagher found him sitting on his bed with his chin sunk in his cupped hands.

"Thomas, you come and eat your supper," she said.

"I don't want any," he answered.

"Please, for my sake."

"Can't you let me alone? You're all against me," he whined.

"I'm your mother!"

"Please, leave me alone. You don't understand."

82

"Now, Thomas . . ." she began.

He walked past her and went into the bathroom. He locked the door. He looked at his eye in the mirror. It was watering, and he touched his handkerchief to it. Pains, coming and going in that region, stabbed him repeatedly. He had never had a shiner like this in all his life. He kept examining it carefully, thinking that the bastards had made his face look like a rainbow. He went back to his room, closed the door, and lay on his bed with a handkerchief over his eyes. Immediately he began to think how it might have been different. They'd been outnumbered. Some of the guys who said they were coming hadn't shown up. Suddenly he was arguing with himself against his brothers. They could let him alone, couldn't they? It wasn't their business.

Maybe he shouldn't have gone Saturday night. He wished he hadn't. He tried to console himself by thinking that he was a martyr, but he couldn't find any consolation in this thought, not with a badge of shame stamped on his face. He was afraid even to go out of the house and let people see it.

He felt a new pain in the eye. He was afraid that he might be permanently disabled.

After his brothers left, he went out to the kitchen and finished his supper. His father came out and sat with him.

"Tommy, tell me what this business is all about. It looks bad to me," Mr. Gallagher said.

"You don't understand."

"Tom, I saw Joe Cannon today. His brother owns a three-story building, and Joe thinks his brother needs a superintendent, and I spoke to him about you getting the job. It's not so much of a job, but after all it's work, and will you take it as soon as you're . . . feeling better?"

Tommy didn't answer. He was fed up with everything here at home. He ate with a brooding look on his face, carefully chewing because of his jaw.

"Will you take it?"

Tommy nodded. He and his father sat in the kitchen, saying nothing.

When the swelling had almost gone, Tommy went to work as the superintendent of the building owned by Joe Cannon's brother. He hated the work, and told himself over and over again that superintendent was a high-toned word for janitor. He had to empty garbage wearing dirty clothes, and this he hated more than any other thing he had to do. And two of the tenants were Jewish. He could scarcely be civil to them. And he kept thinking how in the winter it would be damned cold in the mornings and he'd have to be up early, before dawn, to tend to the furnace. After a week he gave up the work. He decided to go back selling the magazine. After all, it was a cause and it would pay him in the end. Why should he be a dope?

The family was angry and disappointed when they learned that he had given up his new job. He resumed selling *Christian Justice*. He came home one Sunday morning after selling in front of the parish church, feeling glum because he'd had few sales. During the first part of the meal no one talked to him. But Bill and Joe kept glancing at him accusingly. He got sore.

"Cut it out!" he snapped.

"Nobody's saying anything to you," Bill replied.

"I ain't doin' nothin' to you," Tommy said.

"Goddamn you! I'm fed up!" Bill yelled, and he jumped to his feet and rushed around the table.

Tommy started to get out of his chair, but as he was doing so, Bill caught him on the jaw and tumbled him over the chair. Tommy gazed up at Bill, bewildered, holding his jaw. Mrs. Gallagher was on her feet and in tears. Joe and Mr. Gallagher got between Tommy and Bill.

"Fine guy you are, hitting me before I had a chance," Tommy said.

"Shut up, you bum! I'll give you worse than you got!" Bill cried.

Again Joe and the father tried to pacify Bill. They led him back to his chair, and he sat down. Mrs. Gallagher sobbed.

"You wouldn't do that to me outside," Tommy said.

Bill had calmed down. He looked at Tommy scornfully.

"Tommy, your brother lost his temper, but he's

right. You got to turn over a new leaf. You made me look like a monkey running out on the job I got you," Mr. Gallagher said.

"I didn't ask you to do it," Tommy answered.

"Who the hell's going to feed you?" Mr. Gallagher asked, suddenly losing his temper.

"Jesus Christ, but ain't you a nervy sonofabitch," Joe said.

Bill was pushing his chair back. Mrs. Gallagher screamed and yelled out that she would not stand for this. Her tears stopped Bill. While she shook with sobs, Tommy got to his feet.

"All right, if that's the way you feel about it," he said, leaving the room.

Her head bent, Mrs. Gallagher wiped her eyes. The front door was heard to slam.

"He'll come back. That guy likes a meal ticket," Bill said.

"Come now, Mother," the father said as he put his hand tenderly on her shoulder.

"I'm damned glad I socked him," Bill remarked.

87

11

TOMMY was bitter. He walked alone in the milling Sunday night crowd on Broadway, past the lighted theaters where crowds waited in line to be admitted. The brightness of the street, the many people, the atmosphere of pleasure-seeking, all emphasized to him his aloneness. He looked at fellows with girls. He saw a number of foreign or Semitic faces, and every time he saw one, hatred flared in his soul. They were the kind who were to blame for his plight. He smoked his last cigarette and walked with hands stuck in his pockets. Then he wanted another smoke. He thought of bumming the price of a pack off some-one, and he didn't have the nerve to. He told himself again and again that he couldn't go home, he wouldn't. They didn't understand him. He was never going home. They all thought they had him down, did they! Well, they had another guess coming.

Aimless, he wandered along, going over to Fifth Avenue. Many people strolled by, walking slowly, looking in windows, drifting on. A bus stopped beside him, and from the top came the laughter and joshing of two young couples. He looked at them with envy. He strolled along, titillated by shapes of the women who passed. He turned at Forty-second Street and wandered back over to Broadway. He paused in front of a motion picture theater that presented Russian movies, and he cursed Russia and the Reds. He told himself that somebody ought to throw a stink bomb in the place. He wandered on. He picked a cigarette butt off the curb and smoked it. He wandered back to mill along with the slow-moving crowds on Broadway, and to watch the people.

He wandered about Broadway, Seventh Avenue and Fifth Avenue until around midnight. Dismally, he spent his last nickel on subway fare and slumped in a seat in a partially filled subway car. Across from him were several couples on a date, now homeward bound. Seeing fellows with girls like this made him feel more alone. Directly across from him was a tired couple, and the girl rested her blonde head on the fellow's shoulder, while he had his arm around her. A little way down was a good-looking, red-haired girl with a greasy-looking fellow who had a small mustache. They held hands, rubbed knees, and talked low and intently, acting like a couple in love. And he had no girl. And he wanted one. Hell, even if he did have one, he wouldn't have any dough to spend on her. He'd always been a football to be kicked around. He was fed up. His goddamn brother, too, the punk, cracking him when he was sitting down and didn't have a chance to defend himself.

He looked around the car at the couples. His mood changed. He was filled with contempt for those he saw. He wanted to stand up in the car and curse them all with the most obscene words he knew. He dozed off, fell asleep. But luckily he awakened at his station.

He sneaked quietly into the apartment. Bill, who

was in the living room reading the baseball scores in the Monday morning edition of the *News,* heard him come in. Tommy went quietly to his room, quickly took off his clothes, and got into bed. When Bill came into the room to go to bed, Tommy lay with his face to the wall, feigning sleep. Bill looked at him with contempt.

"You haven't even got the guts to sleep in the park," Bill said, beginning to undress.

Tommy pretended not to hear. Making a little noise, Bill finally got undressed, turned the light off, and went to bed. Tommy lay there unable to sleep. He lay awake, pitying himself, telling himself that he was brave, thinking of his hatreds, vowing over and over again that his day was coming, and assuring himself that when it did come, it would be a day of bitter vengeance. Look at Hitler in Germany! Hitler had known days like this, too!